INSIDE OUT

Adapted by Andrea Posner-Sanchez
Illustrated by Alan Batson

🟡 A GOLDEN BOOK • NEW YORK

randomhousekids.com
ISBN 978-0-7364-3629-8 (trade) — ISBN 978-0-7364-3630-4 (ebook)
Printed in the United States of America
10 9 8 7 6 5 4 3

This is Joy. She is an Emotion who lives in
Riley's mind. Ever since Riley was born, Joy
has been in charge of keeping her girl happy.
Joy is very good at her job!

Joy works in Headquarters inside Riley's mind, along with Riley's other Emotions.

Fear helps keep Riley **safe**.

Anger helps Riley express herself if she thinks something is **unfair**—like having to eat broccoli.

Disgust helps Riley stay away from **yucky** things— like broccoli.

And then there is **Sadness**. Joy doesn't understand Sadness. She tries to keep Sadness away from the console—and from Riley's memories.

Joy is proud that most of Riley's memories are happy ones, and she wants to keep them that way!

The most important memories are called **core memories**. They power the **Islands of Personality**—Family Island, Honesty Island, Hockey Island, Friendship Island, and Goofball Island—and make Riley, Riley.

Everything is great until Riley and her family move to a new city. Riley misses her friends, their new house is a mess, and the pizza has **broccoli** on it! Riley's Emotions don't know what to do.

Sadness touches a yellow memory
and it turns blue! When Joy tries to
stop her, all of Riley's core memories
get knocked loose. Joy, Sadness,
and all of the core memories
get sucked out of
Headquarters . . .

. . . and end up lost deep
inside Riley's mind.

Joy is worried. What will happen to Riley if she's not there to make her happy? Joy tries to stay positive. She tells Sadness they need to get back to Headquarters to return the core memories. That's the only way the Islands of Personality will work again.

Things aren't going well back at Headquarters. Without Joy to run things, the other Emotions have to take charge.

Fear, Anger, and Disgust make Riley act different. She's a sore loser at hockey tryouts.

She talks back to her parents.

At school, she sits alone and **sulks**.

Without her core memories in place, Riley's Islands of Personality begin to **crumble** away!

While traveling back to Headquarters, Joy and Sadness run into Riley's old imaginary friend, **Bing Bong**. He is sad because Riley has forgotten him.

Joy is surprised to see that Sadness is able to comfort Bing Bong. Perhaps Sadness is good for something after all.

Meanwhile, Anger gives Riley a terrible idea.
She is going to run away!

On their journey, Joy is surprised to find out that she and Sadness share the same favorite memory. It was after a hockey game back in Minnesota. Sadness remembers that Riley missed the winning shot and felt awful.

Joy replays the memory and sees that Riley
was really sad. But then her family and friends
made her feel better. Joy now understands
that sometimes Riley needs to be sad before
she can be happy again.

Joy and Sadness finally make it back to Headquarters.
And they're just in time—Riley is on a bus!
Joy urges Sadness to take over the console.

All the Emotions watch as Sadness touches the console. Riley begins to feel sad right away. She misses her parents. She yells for the bus driver to stop.

Riley races home. She cries and tells her parents she misses Minnesota. Her parents say they miss Minnesota, too. Riley begins to feel better. She smiles through her tears.

Before long, Riley adjusts to her new life in San Francisco. She has new friends, a new hockey team, and all five Emotions working together as a team.